REDEMPTION AGAINST THE ODDS

RON ROY ROGERS

authorHOUSE®

AuthorHouse™ UK
1663 Liberty Drive
Bloomington, IN 47403 USA
www.authorhouse.co.uk
Phone: 0800.197.4150

© 2017 Ron Roy Rogers. All rights reserved.

No part of this book may be reproduced, stored in a retrieval system, or transmitted by any means without the written permission of the author.

The author has tried to recreate events, locales and conversations from his memories of them. In order to maintain their anonymity in some instances, the author has changed the names of individuals and places. Some identifying characteristics have changed and also details such as physical properties, occupations and places of residence. Any resemblance to actual persons, living or dead, or actual events is purely coincidental.

Published by AuthorHouse   06/19/2017

ISBN: 978-1-5246-8246-0 (sc)
ISBN: 978-1-5246-8245-3 (e)

Print information available on the last page.

Any people depicted in stock imagery provided by Thinkstock are models, and such images are being used for illustrative purposes only. Certain stock imagery © Thinkstock.

This book is printed on acid-free paper.

Because of the dynamic nature of the Internet, any web addresses or links contained in this book may have changed since publication and may no longer be valid. The views expressed in this work are solely those of the author and do not necessarily reflect the views of the publisher, and the publisher hereby disclaims any responsibility for them.

CONTENTS

Introduction 1

Different Situations 3

The Man's Guide to a Broken Heart 7

Shared Experiences 13

Conclusion 87

INTRODUCTION

An insight into the events of two men who in their mid forties find themselves both in a situation of going through a divorce and also showing their difficulties, trials and tribulations during this period and how they help and support each other and overcome their insecurities during a very traumatic period in their lives.

The book is mostly truthful and factual however names and places have been changed to protect all of the people surrounding this colourful story.

Both men have different backgrounds, businesses and lives however their stories are very similar, both have two children (now grown up, well this is open to discussion!) and the common denominator always is :-

IT IS ALWAYS THE MAN'S FAULT and for anyone going through this horrendous experience one thing you do need, is a mate!

To be enlightened please read on but be prepared, this book is not for the feint hearted.

DIFFERENT SITUATIONS

There are quite simply three ways for a relationship or marriage to end – either you dump her, she dumps you or you mutually agree to split.

Unfortunately the latter option is about as common as a snowman in the desert!

Normally one wants it to end and the other does not.

When the female wants it to end and the man does not, you can rest assured she will blame the man for the break up even when she has found someone else, it must make her feel less guilty.

A woman in these situations is like a monkey swinging through the trees, she will only loose the first branch when she has a firm hold on the second branch!

In the cases of the two characters in this book both of whom were on the receiving end of wives who had tried pastures new, one had decided to move on with a new man but keep him in the shadows until her divorce had been finalised, she divorced one of the characters for being unreasonable !

Her new man would then jump out from the shadows into his and her new home which our character had paid for!

The other case came about as a result of his marriage breaking down because he could not accept the deceit and actions shown by his wife and no matter how much he tried to save his marriage the breakdown was inevitable, in cases like this the woman has greater mental strength and when she thinks she has the upper hand, and a new man, her conceit and arrogance is intolerable and very difficult to accept and even more difficult to live with, in fact it can be best described as torturous and whilst he battled on there came a point where he could not take anymore!

To sum up their situations one tried to make it work and the other had no option but to accept his marriage was over and move on as best he could.

It is a good time now to explain that both men were running successful, different businesses and in each case their partners would and did benefit from their husbands' hard work over the years prior to the marriage break ups.

The very first time the two characters who incidentally were old friends, had discussed their private lives was on a trip or a jolly to France to purchase some lower priced booze and cigarettes and their discussions in the car on the way to France were an eye opener for each other as they shared horror stories of their situations for which they both always received the blame, they were each blamed for their wives being unfaithful !

Both wives had cleaners even though they did not work, lived in large houses, had convertible cars such as Mercedes, 4 x 4's, jewellery, meals out and neither wanted for anything yet still they were not satisfied and were both tempted by greener grass.

One wife had an affair with a younger man the other with an older man and I am unsure what reflection this has on our two characters but nonetheless at the time they were each devastated and had to learn to cope with their situations with the help of each other, speaking to each other mostly on a daily basis, frequenting local hostelries in their location and each reciting the menus from memory of their local public houses and restaurants!

Before proceeding any further it is probably best to give our characters names which will be Ron and Reg.

Even now, some 10 years on Ron and Reg regularly meet up, at least weekly, and still discuss their past lives, not all of the time but occasionally, remember it never goes away, you simply learn to live with your past life and get on with your new life, memories become a little faded and some are like they happened yesterday and some are completely forgotten, but one thing is certain you gotta dust yourself down and get back in the race !

Ron's individual experience and their shared experiences will be more detailed a little later on, however a thought for you, before the journey begins :-

"When a man steals your wife, there is no better revenge than to let him bloody well keep her"!

THE MAN'S GUIDE TO A BROKEN HEART

On a serious note when a man is on the receiving end of, shall we say, a difficult time he must learn to accept that times ahead will be tough and you will go through stages of grief, denial, hurt, anger, acceptance and finally elation, one day!

However emotional recovery is not easy and from our experiences you will have the knowledge and benefit as "forewarned is forearmed."

The first thing many of us think when our relationship is over is "she doesn't really mean it."

We are oblivious to danger signs which are obviously in front of us or at least happy to ignore them normally, because of work commitments particularly if you run your own business as you can become embroiled in it, which means the end can come like a bolt from the blue and with no apparent reason, we often think she isn't really serious.

There will be occasions when she isn't serious and is simply giving you a warning, however if she is serious you denying this needs to be replaced with acceptance, or if you want to make it work you need to try to resolve any issues the two of you have before it is too late, either need to happen very quickly because otherwise you will struggle greatly to move on.

You will not be able to escape the pain so there is no point in trying, the intensity will vary depending upon circumstances and there will be times when you will yearn, be in despair, suffer loneliness and a need to vent your anger on something or someone, believe it or not this is quite normal and is all part of the process, not pleasant but a fact of life!

You may, but most likely will not, consider that your ex is not having the time of her life either and she will have to deal with her emotions and feeling miserable due to the failed marriage, however women often deal with the break ups better than men as they are in most cases mentally much stronger than us and women also find it easier to talk it through with their friends, blame the men and "Cry on Shoulders".

In fact, if women were as strong physically as they are mentally us men would all be bloody slaves!

One thing which was glaringly obvious to Ron and Reg was the thankful fact, they had each other to talk to, and please believe it, you do need to talk about it to someone you trust, to keep it to yourself will be painful and not good for your health, it definitely helps and stops some of the heartache and pain, in fact as both were going through the same pains it was rather therapeutic knowing they could help each other.

You will obviously feel anger and the need to blame someone, sometimes it is your fault but only a little, her friend's fault, her family's fault but mostly it is her fault, this may or may not be true (in her eyes you will always be at fault) but it will certainly make you feel better and as long as you do not end up screaming "How could you do this to me, you fucking bitch" at her new bedroom window at 3 O'clock in the morning (or at least not very often) it will make you feel better and there will be time for taking responsibility as you begin to accept the situation.

Our characters have, on occasion been unable to get out of bed in a morning due to the insecurity and sadness they have felt, confidence disappears and is replaced with a feeling of worthlessness, surely if, as was suggested by their wives and they were responsible for the marriage breakdown they would not have these feelings!

When you are constantly told you are useless, no good, do not pay enough attention, spend too much time working or attending business functions you begin to believe some of it !

Eventually, and there is not a time limit for this as we are all different, one morning you will wake up and begin to feel a little better, you realise time and life are continuing for others around you and you have to do the same.

You will not think about her so much, you may even be able to listen to the car radio, it took Ron and Reg at least 6 months to switch the radio on, without a song reminding them of her, you will not want to keep hiding away and you will probably have a conversation with those around you and not mention her which will please them as they are most likely but would not say it, totally pissed off listening to you talking about her, this is the first sign you are beginning to move forward !

You will most likely talk to the opposite sex during work, at the supermarket or in a pub and you will suddenly realise your life is not over and you will flirt with them, which

Redemption Against the Odds

gives you an inner glow/warmth, a little self belief and will make you feel much better, your confidence will begin to return and the only time you will want to stay in bed is ?????? but not there yet!

These are signs that recovery is beginning to show and you will be quite happy to be single and also bear in mind you will have learnt something about yourself, women and relationships but what you must not do is make the same mistakes the next time around!

There is no time limit for the above to happen, as everyone and their situation is different.

Finally after this feeling of acceptance you may well feel a little ecstatic and now you are single anything is possible, start to enjoy life, you can watch football without interruption, leave the duvet ruffled during the day, leave empty beer cans in the lounge waste bin, eat takeaways every night, no nagging, peace around your home, meet the lads for a few beers whenever you feel like it, then suddenly you may be tempted to go on a date but be very careful not to jump in with both feet and suffer what is commonly known as meeting someone

"On the rebound."

When you eventually get over it we suggest you seriously consider the following statement :-

Why get married again quickly? You may as well find a woman you don't like and buy her a fucking house!

SHARED EXPERIENCES

Reg had already left the matrimonial home and had for a few years lived like a gipsy moving from place to place, in fact we fully expected him to have his ears pierced!

Ron on the other hand stayed at the house with his family until the bitter end, having been dragged away from his dream home kicking and screaming, uttering only expletives to his wife during the time it took to sell the house, for what she had done to the family and himself, not that he wanted her to suffer because he only mentioned it about fifty times a day.

Ron had a customer who had a house he wanted to rent out for a twelve month period at about the same time as he had to move out of his home as it had now been sold, Reg also at this time needed to move out of his rented shed as his lease had expired and Winter was on its way!

To add to their woes Ron's Nineteen year old daughter did not want to live with her Mother and boyfriend so decided to move on and in with Dad and Reg to add some light entertainment to their dull lives !

Reg moved in a few weeks before Ron and Daughter, thankfully he had cutlery, crockery and furniture because Ron, had nothing at all, but at least he had his mate to talk to.

The house had only two bedrooms so daughter, who we will call Ronetta, had the dining room which was spacious enough to be kitted out as a bedroom, and Ron and Reg had their own bedrooms upstairs.

As mentioned earlier winter was almost upon us so the central heating was switched on and lasted for three days, the fucking oil ran out !

A top-up of the tank was requested and arrived five days later, in the interim electric blow heaters were purchased and placed strategically around to stop ice forming inside the house!

The oil arrived and now the fucking boiler would not start!

Reg, having had some experience with engines managed to get it working thankfully, and the fan heaters were put into storage until the next time the oil ran out as the level on the tank was bust!

Being men, the two ate out on a regular basis in fact it was so regular it was every bloody day, don't think they left out Ronetta as she ate mostly at her boyfriend's house, his mother was a decent cook!

One of the secret's of getting through a situation like this is to believe you are never on your own or the only one going through it, our fame as new divorcee's was beginning to spread and our regular Sunday afternoon haunt where we always ate, naturally after several pints of fine ale, started to receive an influx of men experiencing the same and at its height we had a table for fifteen eating late Sunday lunch.

The age difference between all of us was only about five years, and we would share jokes and stories of our experiences, which revolved around the wife buggering off with someone else and blaming the men for their deceit and infidelity, in fact they will rarely admit the truth but believe us a woman does not end her marriage unless she has found someone else!

The cost of a divorce was often discussed and whilst we all felt screwed we knew the solicitors costs were horrendous and have you seen the internet where divorces are advertised from £37.00 upwards, what a load of cobblers that is!

We all experienced legal costs in the thousands!

Reasons for divorce's, no-one cares, it is all about one party screwing the other and the Lawyer getting paid a fucking fortune for ruining, in most cases a blokes life, the Lawyer and in our experiences the judge, do not give a damn whose fault the breakdown is, just screw him for as much as you can.

Blaming the man for the breakdown of all of our marriages was normal :-

"It was your fault I had three affairs, you didn't pay me enough attention", the poor bastard worked ten hours a day, she didn't work, regularly had her hair and nails done, had new clothes, drove a new car and kids at private school, how on earth could it be his fault?

"I would be happy living in a caravan with you if you didn't work so many hours" what a fucking stupid thing to say when we all know she didn't mean it.

"I need a break(doesn't work, two kids age seven and nine) so I am going to Spain with Ruth (her single friend, two failed marriages) because we have only had one holiday this year! He runs a small engineering business employing four people and has to look after his kids as well for two weeks.

Self first, second and last, and it is his fault she needs a break!

Some women, and we use the word some, we dare not say most, believe themselves to be special and above the rest of us, if they only supported their hard working husbands their lives in the long term could be idyllic, but there is now't so blind as those who can't see, or those who do not want to see.

Women are very naive in some scenarios seeing only what they want to see and believing the grass is greener elsewhere, we have a bit of advice for women who are like that .....

"Don't look up to, or aspire to be like, or compare yourself to others, they are normally more screwed up than you can possibly imagine."

Back at Ron and Reg's rented palace, Ronetta, who was aspiring to be a model and currently at college, decided to start a diet called the Atkins diet where she only ate fried foods which lasted for a month.

Every time Ron and Reg came home from work or the pub, mostly the pub as they didn't go home at night just straight to the pub, the house smelt like a fucking transport cafe and we think she was teaching them how to wash up, as if they needed any practise, because she would leave the dirty pots and pans as a present for them !

In fact they were rarely at the house in the day because of work commitments however Ron used to pop back a few times every week to meet the ironing lady, just to make sure she was ok!

After a while, Reg who must have been feeling lonely and suffering from excessive alcoholic intake, decided to get a dog so he had to go back to the house and not the pub at the end of the working day to feed the dog (boring bastard).

Redemption Against the Odds

Ron, after losing his early doors drinking partner decided to get his own back!

One Saturday they both decided where they would eat that night and Reg, who enjoys his food, decided to have a rest and a snooze on the afternoon, Ron on the other hand had a day with the boys "having a few shandys" or "sherberts "and when he had enough to drink he wasn't bothered about eating, Reg arrived early that evening, ready and looking forward to have something to eat, took one look at Ron and said "you're not hungry are you" Ron simply smiled, and whilst the two have never fallen out or had any serious crosswords Reg called him everything he could think of beginning with .... you f................................!

Ron went to check out the ironing lady and let Reg cool off !

The dog was a nice little pup and settled in well with the three of them, Ronetta making a big fuss of it whenever she was around.

She wasn't the tidiest of young ladies, in fact she was bloody scruffy but the two grown ups never interfered and left her and her room alone in fact the ironing lady sometimes tidied up her room for her but only if she had a few hours to spare !

Reg's cousin Ray often called round and went out quite regularly with Ron and Reg for a pint or two and accompanied them on one of their regular jollies to France for a few days, the one day he called around early evening, Ron was obviously at the pub and Reg was frantically searching for the dog who had disappeared, they both searched and eventually heard whimpering from Ronetta's bedroom, the dog had pushed the door open but it had closed behind her, Reg opened the door to let the dog out and said to Ray "Fuckin' Hell we've been burgled, look at the fuckin' mess they've made in this room". They began looking around to see where entry was gained but could not find anything, they looked outside for footprints by all of the windows and doors but still found nothing, Ronetta arrived home before Ron, and Reg apologised to her for going in to her room and explained they had been broken into but were struggling to find out how or where entry had been gained, Ronetta ran to check her room and came

Redemption Against the Odds

back happily to say everything was ok and was just as she left it !

They went many times to France and were always stopped by the custom's officials in fact one year they were stopped on their way out of England!

The customs must have thought they had pinched Ron's Mercedes and they do look a little bit menacing however it proves you can never judge a book by it's cover!

Another time they were accompanied by two aquaintances and they had each purchased a box of cigarettes, as they were usually stopped they waited in the queue for the officials to pull them over and right on cue they were directed into a building to be checked.

The officer asked Reg what they had purchased and he said a box of cigarettes each, obviously not believing Reg the boot of the car was opened and we heard the official say "fucking hell I thought you meant a carton each not a fucking shopful" each box contained 25 cartons of 200 cigarettes.

We were taken out of the car and our passports were taken to be checked…?

By the time they returned to us one of our group had emptied the shelves of the free lighters given to people who purchased cigarettes in France and who had obviously had them and the lighters confiscated!

When he got back in the car he struggled to sit down as the lighters were sticking in to him, we stopped at the services and he emptied his pockets of 72 cigarette lighters!

They gave us back our passports and the cigarettes and told us to have a safe journey back home!

On another occasion the two visited Ostend with a business acquaintance, they normally went to France for their short breaks but thought this would make an interesting change and bloody hell it was interesting, their acquaintance was into visiting massage parlours and in Ostend there are plenty to choose from !

Ron and Reg have never been interested in participating and had never visited one before !

Their eyes were well and truly opened as their companion took them into one and it was like a small drinking bar, 3 beers were brought to the table and after one large swig he went to choose a girl and disappeared, to, Ron and Reg assumed a private room, however after a few minutes they heard a noise coming from behind a curtain in the bar and then more noise and groans !

At this point Ron and Reg were feeling a little uncomfortable but also highly amused at the noises he was making, they thought about leaving but were worried he may get mugged so they sat there until they heard one almighty groan from him signalling he had finished, he then walked from behind the curtain, stark bollock naked, stood at the table and finished his beer!

He naturally got dressed before joining Ron and Reg to continue their evening, but nothing could surpass the unrepeatable entertainment they had experienced and they doubt if anything ever will!

During this period, in the lives of our two downtrodden characters many things were going on, a few years prior to their new found bachelor existence they had a joint business venture and purchased a local public house and believe it or not, the beer swilling entrepreneurs knocked it down !

Some people thought they were losing the plot!

However, not these two, they built nine starter homes on the plot and at the height of the last property boom sold them all, having taken the Mayor out for a good night helped, he used to go to the same youth club as Ron and Reg in their younger days and planning permission was easily granted!

Whilst they were still running their own respective businesses they were looking for something else to roll their latest generated income into, and just to prove to all around them they had not lost their love of the amber nectar, good times and the opposite sex (when they moved in to the rented house some folk thought hey up, what's going on here, but dare not ever say anything) they purchased an old country club which had bars, a restaurant, night club, gym, outdoor lido (that is a swimming pool for those of you who are thick) letting rooms and plenty of land in a beautiful rural setting which generated an abundance of beautiful women who were all upper class, we spotted this immediately when viewing the place because their tattoo's were spelt correctly!

A club of this size was very difficult for one person to look after, this soon became apparent after we found Reg trying to strangle the manager after he had messed up on a number of occasions.

Many managers were tried from single women, single men, a couple who lived free at the club, a drunken alcoholic bar manger and his cat, a gym manager who enjoyed phoning Aunty Shiela and Uncle Bruce.

Ron Roy Rogers

We were surrounded by useless arse's who didn't want to work hard and were fiddling, where there is cash, booze and tobacco everyone likes at least two of them so we were double fucked, we knew it but could not prove it.

We bet you won't believe this one – one night Ron arrived at the club and spoke to the chef as he was throwing a black bin bag into the waste skip, pleasantries were exchanged and Ron went in to meet Reg as they were meeting someone later that evening. Meals had finished, the chef and waitresses went home and the duo's business colleague arrived as expected, they were chatting over a sociable drink when their colleague said "you'll never guess what I just saw as I was getting out of my car, a bloke with blue and white striped trousers taking a bin bag "out" of your skip.

The fucking chef was thieving from us as well, taking meat etc., to the waste skip and retrieving it when leaving for the day !

Meeting finished, Reg got pissed and Ron went to check out his ironing!

Gordon applied for the job but we told him to "fuck off" because of his bad language.

Add to cash, booze and tobacco---FOOD!

We were both well and truly peed off, we couldn't trust our wives or our staff, only each other.

We also had staff at our respective businesses which were both long established with employees we thought we could trust and rely upon, how wrong we both were, obviously not all of the staff were untrustworthy, liars, thieves, cheats and generally no good bastards, just a couple in each of our businesses, but we think it best to save up these stories for another short book (already underway)

Trust takes years to build but only suspicion to destroy !

Back at the transport cafe/palace/rented house Ron and Reg licked their wounds and coughed up another £5,000 each to plough into the club to cover the discrepancies.

The newest of the new managers came up with an idea to transform the place and spend £80,000 to give it a facelift....................PLONKA !

They did give it a noticeable facelift which cost around £5,000 and it looked very nice, neat and contemporary, they liked it, anyway.

The club had the only 2.00am drinking licence for miles around and at one of our management meetings the resident disc jockey suggested shutting at 1.00am, not thinking about losing another hour's takings, Reg nearly strangled him as well, at least his throat was better for the disco that night, needless to say he didn't stay for long afterwards.

They had a company van used to fetch and carry items for the lido, gym, bar and restaurant, it was on lease and was costing about £300 per month, no-one could ever really answer this question, "how did the cleaner get her hands on the van and use it for over a fucking year?"

So there they were being screwed constantly, losing money and the fucking cleaner was driving around in a company vehicle.

No wonder some folk thought they had lost the plot.

After losing the latest manager it was decided one of them had to be the liquer licence holder in order to maintain continuity of the business whilst a proper manager was sought............!

As usual Reg came up with the advice and Ron was heading back to college for a day's intense course all about being a licencee and taking his exam the following day whilst trying to blot out thoughts of his impending appearances in court regarding his divorce.

A week later Ron discovered he had passed his exam and became licencee of the club with Reg confirming his advice "Told you it would be ok, you're better at things like that than I am"

Ron soon realised Reg didn't enjoy hard work as he had spent his early years grafting as a mechanic working on heavy goods vehicles and when there was work to be done at the club Reg always turned up when it was finished earning him the nickname "blister" as he always arrived after the work was finished!

Being a licencee doesn't end there as Ron soon found out and had to attend court every time the club needed to extend it's licencing hours for entertainment, weddings, parties and the like.

The first time Ron went to the licencing court he took the club's solicitor who he had only met briefly once before, with him.

It was a particularly bad time for Ron as his marriage break up had unnerved him greatly and his confidence was also at an all time low, Ron was rather upset on the way to the court in the car with this poor solicitor who must have thought he had drawn the short straw having ended up with a lunatic on the way to a licencing court to obtain an extension to licencing hours under the control of this man who was struggling to control himself!

It actually turned out to be the start of a professional relationship which developed into mutual respect and a good friendship, in fact he asked them to take him to Ostend, but they declined!

Ron soon began going to the licencing court himself and the club saved on paying extortionate legal costs!

Despite the setbacks at the club they thoroughly enjoyed the roller coaster journey it gave them, they hosted gentlemen's evenings with guest speakers from the world of sport including ex world champion boxers, European cup winning and premier league winning footballers along with a comedian and attractive dancing ladies at each event.

Tribute bands were also great fun and one was to be held in our marquee around the pool in June as

Redemption Against the Odds

obviously we tried to pick the best weather for such events.

This was the first time they had attempted erecting their own marquee and after much sweat and tears and a collective effort of about 8 bodies it was finally completed two days after the procedure had started, "blister" arrived and said it looked good!

They were all very excited and looking forward to Saturday when the event was to be held, it was Wednesday evening when they had finished the completion and all headed home to rest after the hard work of erecting the marquee.

At 9.00am the following morning Reg's son had arrived at the club and saw the marquee damaged beyond recognition, it was totally fucking destroyed, there had been a very violent storm on the Wednesday evening and the canvasses had been ripped, the weight of the water had brought most parts of it down and the framework twisted like paperclips.

In order for the event to still go ahead we found a company to hire a marquee from and they were extremely good and erected it on the Friday and the function went ahead as planned.

They then began an insurance claim to recover some of their losses however the amount received was not enough to warrant purchasing their own marquee so they decided to continue to hire them and put the money in the bank to be swallowed up by everyone there who was fiddling!

You can imagine at this time Ron and Reg were utterly pee'd off but as they have always done, they bounced back and Reg almost had a smile on his face.

Also weddings were held in our new contact's hired marquees, in fact Reg's son held his wedding

Redemption Against the Odds

reception at the club which was very entertaining for Ron and Reg as they were the only people who were sober (not lying cos they were both driving)

Reg's soon to be ex gave him a few scowling looks especially when a rather attractive but loud guest draped her leg over his shoulder and around his neck and blew her referee's whistle many times and very loud, she had bloody long legs all the way up they went, Ron didn't notice the stockings or thong – Reg told him the following day, Ron was gutted!

Ron's daughter held her 18th at the club and again this was entertaining, however this time Ron wasn't sober and was thoroughly enjoying himself, his ex-wife, whose boyfriend was afraid to come, kept glaring at him every time he danced with a spelt correctly tattoo'd beauty and of course the ironing lady.

As one would expect she rallied her friends around and just kept scowling and glaring at Ron. Surprisingly none of her friends spoke to him? even some of her friends husbands would not speak to him, a lot of them are now divorced and the cheeky bastards have rung Ron for help and/or advice, some folk have got more front than Sainsburys, we used to say Woolies but they've gone now!

On reflection about the club, they know, had their circumstances been different they would not have sold it and would have most probably lived there, but there you go, three years flew by and another chapter closed.

If you got no socks on you can't pull 'em up !

By God you could never say their lives were dull and uneventful !

Life after the club was strangely quiet and they had a chance to take things a little easier, they went out socially to more places, jollies to France became more frequent, they even managed to go to the Monte Carlo Grand Prix and in the same year squeezed in watching Mike Tyson defeat Julian Francis in Manchester, his only fight in England, along with the last England game at the old Wembley Stadium, when Kevin Keegan ran away, again!

Being normally hard working fellas they realised this high life could not continue indefinitely and Ron asked Reg if his company could do a conversion job on a commercial property he owned into apartments which he did and Ron and his kids still own them and rent them out.

Reg purchased a pub in a nice little village close to where they were living and he now rents it out, after trying a number of managers who all turned out to be drunks or tossers, in fact the reminder of the days at the club came flooding back, so renting it out became the least stressful option!

Reg, being more deep than Ron finds it difficult to recall the hurt, anger and sadness, and to put into words what his experiences were along with the impact they had on him, but it is reasonable to say he was gutted and devastated by the situation he found himself in and what helped him was his ability to help Ron get through the bloody awful mess he was in and this obviously took his mind off his own problems.

As you will discover Ron needed plenty of help!

It has been nine years since Ron's divorce and to put into words and write down the events, build up and circumstances, has proved to be more painful than he anticipated, as you recall one situation it leads on to something else and so on.

The beginning is a good place to start, but Ron's story does not have a definitive start but most certainly a definitive ending!

The start in his ex's eyes was when she told Ron on Christmas Day she wanted a divorce, because he did not show her enough attention or affection, worked too many hours and did not do what a "normal family" does, whatever that is, after she had spent an hour on the telephone speaking to her boyfriend whilst the kids opened their presents!

She used to say "you only want sex when you've been drinking" not true, sometimes Ron wanted a kebab and chips or a curry!

She enjoyed all of the finer things in life that came as a result of hard work by Ron, clothes, jewellery, home help, nice cars, nice home – you get the jist of it, but as she always needed to be the centre of attention it was never good enough for her.

When Ron bought a Rolex watch for their daughter on her eighteenth birthday all his wife said was "I had to wait until I was Forty before I had one".

She, rather pathetically, called for the kids, Ron and his parents to be at the house at 7.00pm one night in March, where she informed everyone there, without any consideration shown towards the children, she had filed for a divorce, nice !

Ron received his letter from her solicitor the following day!

Yesterday, nine years on Ron went to see one of his client's in North Wales, an annual trip where he always took Ray one of his close and good friends

Redemption Against the Odds

however he passed away six months ago so Ron felt a real sadness as he drove to his meeting. The Company he was going to see was formed approximately 35 years ago and Ron, his Wife and Daughter met the Founder of the Company and his Wife whilst on holiday in the Canary Islands 21 years ago.

The Founder of the business actually sold it to his Manager approximately ten years ago and moved to Spain where he and his wife have lived ever since.

At the meeting with the previous Manager, now the owner and has become a good friend of Ron's, Ron asked how the previous owner was as he had not spoken to him for a few years and was then informed that he had passed away only ten days ago.

Ron and his wife after having met the couple in question actually purchased a holiday home in the area as a result of their friendship and after his meeting he went to look at the now sold holiday home, saw trees and shrubs he had planted, it brought back memories which perhaps he had chosen to forget.

He decided to park his vehicle and take a walk on the beach to blow the cobwebs away and clear his head as memories came flooding back.

The point Ron is making is even though it has been nine years and he has moved on there are still moments when you cannot stop the memories or the hurt that comes with them, you simply have to live with them and carry on.

It's called Life!

Back in 1999 Ron's wife who blamed him constantly for anything and everything that went wrong decided to come clean about her alcohol addiction, which was also Ron's fault, and spent a month at the local expensive well known clinic allegedly drying out, at a cost of £20,000, obviously to Ron.

The build up to this admission included damaging various cars on a regular basis, causing trouble with friends, family and the local school and if anyone knows an alcoholic you will be aware that they struggle greatly to tell the truth, in fact the week before going into the clinic she disappeared for five days, starting the day after Boxing Day, on a bender sleeping on someone's settee but she would not say who or where, she returned home once during this period to collect some clean clothes and their six year old son, upon seeing his Mom called out to her and put his arms out, she turned her back on him and walked away, I wonder what long term effect this may have on him?

Redemption Against the Odds

During this 5 day period Reg and his cousin Ray called to see Ron, to see if he was ok, Reg had a cup of tea and Ray had a whisky which Ron poured directly from the bottle, Ray spat it out uttering "what the fuck is that" it was actually cold tea and after checking the other bottles they were all filled with cold tea, whisky, brandy and sherry, with water in the vodka and gin bottles!

They then asked if he wanted to go to a party, "where?" asked Ron, they both replied "a jump in the cut party" They were all in the throes of separations/divorces and were all equally pee'd off but at least saw the funny side of jumping in the canal.(looking back, not really funny is it?)

When she eventually returned it was New Years Eve and she had spoken to her G.P. and informed Ron she was booked into, with the G.P.'s help, a very expensive clinic and was to be admitted that evening. Ron along with his father in law, took her to the clinic and at midnight she had gone to her room and the two of them were seated in the reception area !

Four words were uttered between them....

Happy Fucking New Year!

What a nonsense that was !

Having left the clinic after a month, where Ron with the help of his parents coped with the children and the household chores, her cleaner/ironing lady was nowhere to be seen, she was ladened with bottles of pills to ease the cravings and stop the addictions?

From one drug to another!

She started attending alcoholics anonymous held two evenings a week at the Clinic.

Naturally, during this time Ron constantly received the blame for her being an alcoholic for not giving her enough attention or treating her properly, however he regularly picked up the pieces as a result of her actions and the mess she left in her wake.

She used to chew parsley to try to hide the smell of the alcohol so when Ron came home from work she would stand there, swaying, and saying I haven't had a drink today, with bits of green stuck to her teeth, quite funny if you are not on the receiving end of it!

One early evening in the summer she returned home with their son at about 5.30pm and virtually fell out of her 4 x 4 and promised to stop drinking again as she struggled to stand up and was swaying with green bits of parsley on her teeth, an insult again to Ron's intelligence and putting their son's life and other road user's lives at risk, again !

She didn't work and had a cleaner/ironing lady (not Ron's ironing lady) 5 days a week, who had to be at their house for 8.30am to take their son to school and she would ask anyone to pick him up and bring him home because she was always too drunk, however, if it was something for herself she would drive regardless of her intake of alcohol, this caused Ron great concern particularly for the safety of her passengers and other road users, there were always new dents appearing on her car and Ron would have to fork out again for it to be repaired, she did from time to time have to return a "picking up of a child favour", she obviously hid her state of mind and body very well because if the other parents knew they would have been horrified, or maybe some of them knew and turned a blind eye because she had their sympathy!

Now't so strange as folk!

Ron had to come home from work one day because a member of her family had called to see her at 11.00am and could not get in, she looked through the window and could see her lying on the sofa and their 2 yr old son sitting on the floor in his pyjamas, the family member thought she was ill, but when Ron let her in it transpired, as Ron already knew, she was drunk as a skunk!

After attending for a number of months at the AA venue she became more involved and started playing golf with the other drunks, I mean alcoholics, she even became a "Born again Christian" need I say any more, in fact she was more fucking screwed up now than when she was drinking !

At least she could now drive her car without hitting as many things as before !

Ron remembers one occasion prior to going into the Clinic where he cooked a slap up Sunday breakfast which he and the kids sat down to and he went upstairs to call his wife and found her at ten o'clock in the morning sitting on the bed talking on the telephone and swigging a bottle of whisky!

What a sorry state to be in, Ron took the bottle out of her hand and poured it down the toilet while she started screaming and shouting at Ron to leave her alone, he had not touched her – just removed the bottle from her – all done for effect and sympathy for who ever was on the end of the phone and saying what a bastard Ron was because he had just attacked her !

One time Ron arrived home with the children as he had collected them from his parents after work, to find her drunk and asleep on the floor in their daughter's bedroom, sad sorry sights like this are commonplace when your partner is an alcoholic and in a lot of cases, even worse !

When drink takes over anything can, and does happen!

One year when the kids were younger they went on a family holiday to Southern France with friends and their child, Ron and his friend drove, in order they had a vehicle when they were there to visit places and the wives and children flew, Ron and his friend were to collect them from the Airport which they did but they almost missed the flight from the U.K. because his wife was not ready on time!

You would have thought she had learned a lesson however on the return home they did miss the flight and managed to arrive home a day late, drink causing havoc again!

Another flight and holiday, for her brother's Carribean wedding, (without Ron) she left a piece of hand luggage with the camera and other belongings on the plane, which were never recovered, Ron doubts she even took them on the plane, if she could have ever told the truth she would not know or remember.

Her Father who was also at the wedding told Ron she was drunk most of the time causing havoc and arguments and became rather friendly with the piano player!

Not really a surprise!

As time went on she became more involved with the AA and the functions they had, meetings, discussion groups etc., Ron noticed his bank balance had reduced on a regular basis over a period of three/four months and when he confronted her about it her response was quite simply :-

"Would you prefer it if I were drinking"!

Ron occasionally collected their son from school and always struggled to understand why none of the parents, particularly the mothers, would ever speak to him and in fact totally ignored him, it was quite obvious they had been told stories by his wife about him in order for her to have people on her side and to have their sympathy, which she craved along with attention.

Their son had a severe hearing loss from birth, apparently caused because he was born 11 weeks premature (as a result of her alcohol and drug abuse?) and she always played on this and joined various support groups who help handicapped kids, Ron went along with this for a while but saw his son (who incidentally could speak perfectly well and clear without any impediment and appeared to have

Redemption Against the Odds

no major problem in hearing things) mixing with, attending parties with, group outings, sporting activities and other support group activities which for a child without a handicap must be a little unnerving.

Ron's wife used to be a nurse so Ron accepted all she said about their son's hearing, however when Ron started taking him to the hospital after his wife was incapable, for his six monthly check ups he asked the consultant about his son's hearing loss, fearing the worst Ron and son sat together and listened to an explanation in simple English how his son had a SLIGHT, not severe hearing loss !

She had even registered him as disabled!

All done for sympathy, attention and what Ron eventually found out – money, in the form of disability allowance and carer's allowance, of which Ron was blissfully unaware, with the money being spent on herself and (read on) !

After about twelve months Ron felt rather uneasy because things were happening to him which he did not quite understand such as money going from the account, his wife spending most of her time out at meetings, discussion groups, going away for weekends on so called Born Again Christian functions leaving him basically as, a single parent whilst also trying to run two businesses.

Ron's suspicious nature led him to bug the telephones at home (he always wanted to be James Bond!) and upon playing back some of the phone calls it was blatantly obvious that something was going on between her and a volunteer counsellor who is also a drunk and to top it all he is a fucking jock!

Ron then had a private detective follow the two of them and it was confirmed by the detective that she was having an affair, with video evidence to prove this, not very pleasant seeing your wife shagging in a car on the car park of the AA meeting venue.

When she returned home Ron asked her where she had been, she blatantly lied to him and when he confronted her with the truth she started screaming and shouting accusing him of attacking her and she called the Police. Four Policemen arrived to arrest Ron and take him away, their Daughter stood up and said to the Police "Why are you here my Dad has not done anything"

God Bess Her!

The Police left and that was the end of the alleged matter. However, Ron was arrested a few more times as a result of her lies which will be mentioned later.

A few days later she admitted to her affair to Ron and Ronetta, and he found out where the money had gone, it had paid to furnish a flat she and the Volunteer Counsellor had rented in a village about 15 miles away, and when Ron and his family thought that she was at the AA meetings or Born Again Christian weekends/meetings she was obviously at this flat or staying in hotels with her boyfriend, again paid for by Ron.

It was quite easy for Ron to track the boyfriend down and find out where he lived, with Reg's help they followed one of the other drunks one night and knocked on the door of his flat, he was a rather scruffy, untidy looking fella who spoke awfully posh and was rather pompous, arrogant and hostile towards them, he did not want to talk to them or tell them anything about Ron's wife or the jock but after he was dangled over the balcony of his flat he told them more than they needed to know, in fact they could not shut him up!

He did live on the 10th floor!

She hated admitting the truth, as the truth did not agree with her and she called Ron a "fat ugly bastard" to which Ron responded "that isn't very nice" and she apologised and said "I meant to say you fat ugly bald bastard"

Ron could never understand when other fella's he knew who said they did not know their wife was having an affair, he used to say :-

"Surely you must have known, I would have"

He didn't !

Redemption Against the Odds

Naturally all of this was Ron's fault and divorce proceedings were issued against Ron as he was "UNREASONABLE"!

Ron decided to stay at the home and endured the mental torture of seeing his wife dress herself up to go out at night whilst he looked after their son and daughter, in fact on a couple of occasions Ron thought they may even reconcile their differences and move on with the marriage however it was never to be.

On one particular occasion she asked Ron to kiss her to see if he was as good as her boyfriend and to see if she still had any feelings for him!

Ron being an absolute fucking idiot went along with this and after he had given her a long lingering kiss she smirked and looked him straight in the eye and said "No I don't think so"

Humiliated and hurt do not really describe his feelings by her response.

Everything was back to normal the following day as she threw a knife at him and he ducked as the the knife flew past his ear and beheaded a bizzy lizzy plant!

One day a friend of Ron's took him Pigeon Shooting and when Ron returned home obviously his wife was not there, his kids were with his Parents so Ron decided to clean his gun having used it all day, his wife returned home, saw him cleaning his gun and again rang the police to say he was going to shoot her.

The thought had never crossed his mind............!

To this the police responded in great numbers, saw what Ron was doing and told his wife not to be quite so dramatic and to leave him alone.

As a result of this incident some of their son's friends were not allowed to visit to play with him!

Obviously it was not the police who told their parents about it!

The police saga does not end there as a few weeks later Ron was with his kids on a Sunday afternoon and his wife returned home at approximately 2.00pm and started screaming and shouting at Ron as usual for some unknown reason, and went out again, she rang the police, from wherever she had gone and told them that Ron had assaulted her and this time the police thinking there was no smoke without fire took Ron into custody, his wife stayed away from the house leaving the kids on their own to watch their Dad being driven away in a police car, luckily Ron's parents again came to the rescue and stayed with them until their mother decided to return home.

Ron knew a number of the local policemen and in fact when he was taken into the Police Station he knew the Duty Sargeant who was an old footballing colleague and they had an "Off the Record" chat and a policeman Ron had never met before actually took time to talk to him, took a statement and confirmed that he would be reporting to his Superior that no further action should be taken.

This was simply due to the fact that his wife had stated he had punched her in the face and as Ron is six foot one and seventeen stone and his wife did not have a mark on her face it was obvious that she was lying, again!

She was warned about wasting police time.

The policeman took Ron home and again an "Off the Record" chat took place whereby he informed Ron to be extremely careful as his wife was like a loose cannon, in other words totally unreliable, screwed up and a fucking maniac, the policeman's words were – "a very dangerous woman."

Her boyfriend who obviously had not got a pot to pee in, was making all of the bullets for her to fire so he could have an easy life on Ron's hard earned, being a drunk he obviously had no job except for volunteering to help out at AA and prey on impressionable, vulnerable women to try to obtain an easy life for himself.

Ron could not help but pay him a couple of visits and he will not be preying on any more vulnerable women again!

The first time Ron almost caught him but he ran into the house he was intending to share with Ron's ex and hid behind a chair as Ron was banging on the door and window, Ron was rather angry at this because his divorce had not yet been finalised and Ron purchased this house for his ex and Roger because he did not want any more disruption in Roger's life and to see her boyfriend there helping to put things in the house pissed him off, a little !

Never mind…………………… "Beware the wrath of a patient man"

This obviously now leads on to the final time Ron was arrested, this was in the area where the boyfriend lived after Ron's visit to him, the policeman spoke to his counterpart in the area where Ron lived and he also had an "Off the Record" chat with Ron and told him to stay cool and not to go anywhere near the boyfriend again, he also confirmed he thought the boyfriend was a complete Ass and deserved everything he received!

Ron did arrange for another surprise for him after he came out of hospital, a visit by a rather large man who asked if he was feeling better to which he replied "Yes" he was then told he would be back in hospital if he pursued any criminal damage claim against Ron, and for a much longer and more painful period!

During this time Ron luckily had the support of his Parents who were really too old to have to put up with Shit like this (if they read this they won't be very happy with me for saying that) but were extremely supportive of their grandchildren and him.

They say a leopard does not change its spots and once an alcoholic always an alcoholic and when you find drink hidden all over the house including your young son's bedroom, whisky, brandy and sherry bottles filled with cold tea, gin and vodka bottles filled with water, it becomes normal and a way of life, for them to lie constantly.

They say a story is always good until the TRUTH is told!

Luckily for Ron the majority of people she tried to con did not believe her fairy stories and those who did were obviously on the same wave length as her, God help them!

Ron met some of the screwed up alcoholics and was amazed how the vast majority of them were so full of their own self importance and the belief they held that they were above the rest of us and were special.

She had two female friends whom Ron met and both were screwing around with other addicts and their poor husbands who were paying for their treatment were being taken advantage of by these "special women" who did not believe they were doing anything wrong!

If a pig is born in a cow shed... it's still a pig.

Ron did not live like a monk during this period and apart from the ironing lady, he had a few other conquests, and noticeably none of them drank too much either!

Sadly none of them were nymphomaniacs, rich or owned a public house, but they were all younger than Ron!

The divorce finally arrived about 18 months after it began, she was awarded a lot and Ron fuck all!

Redemption Against the Odds

Whilst the divorce was going on Ron was instructed by his Solicitor not to change anything such as bank accounts and the like!

This allowed her to take full advantage of this ludicrous instruction and she bought all brand new bed linen, towels and cutlery for her new home with Ron's earnings!

In fact Ron left the matrimonial home without so much as a knife and fork!

He now had to pick himself up, dust himself down and get back in the race not only for his own sake but for his son and daughter, and now is the time you discover exactly, who is a friend and who is an Ass, and he promises and guarantees, whoever you are, there are many more Asses than friends !

Ron, along with his daughter and best mate Reg moved into a rented house at the beginning of October at a time in each of their lives which was very messed up and hard to get used to.

Being men of principal, hard working and having morals and scruples, life began to settle down and they were soon into a routine, which rubbed off on Ronetta and she soon had a part time job to help her through college, and a boyfriend who helped her through this traumatic period of her life.

In fact she spoke more to Ron during the twelve months they were at the rented house than she ever did previously and recalled how on the rare occasions Ron had a meal at the matrimonial home prepared for him she had done it!

Not right for a young girl aged from twelve to seventeen to do this or even witness the mess her mother had created for her own selfish reasons.

Very sad.

She also told Ron since the age of twelve she used to hide all of the empty bottles and cans before Ron arrived home from work.

The cleaner left at 1.00pm each day and her mother would then start to openly drink, anything, but mostly strong cider and spend all of the afternoon talking on the telephone and getting rapidly pissed.

After she had moved in with Ron she went to see her mother once a week and never once did her mother call Ron to check how she was getting on.

When Ronetta finished school and had received an award to be presented to her at the Town Hall, Ron attended with her boyfriend and the three of them went out for a Cantonese meal afterwards to celebrate, her mother said she had to do something and could not go with them.

When they returned home her Mother was drunk on the settee!

Ron went to all of her parents evenings, attended all of her presentations and took her to school and college every day from the age of seven or eight up until she passed her driving test.

They were and still are very close, and she loved Uncle Reg but doesn't see him very often now as she has moved to London and when she returns home to visit it is always a "flying visit". She often recalls some of the good times (in a sad situation) they all shared at their rented pad and the good lessons and values she learnt including playing darts in a public house one Saturday afternoon until early evening, none of them could really play and got worse as time went on!

At this time Ron had been checked out by the CSA who gave their recommendation to the court and had to pay maintenance for his son to his ex-wife in the sum of £840.00 per month even though Ron had three nights and two days access, per week!

No wonder the CSA are frowned upon, another bunch of faceless government employees who have not got a clue about real life and live in the same cuckoo world as social workers who always get their paycheck at the end of the month even though they never earn it and regularly drop clangers and get away with it !

Ron's glad he has got that off his chest !

Ron struggled in the beginning with the access to his son and found it very upsetting to take him home after his day or two visit, but time helps to overcome this but the pain is always there, you just have to, and learn to, live with it.

His son, from reading between the lines, also found it difficult because he didn't really know this new found Scottish drunk (well he was sober then but remember the leopard whose spots don't change!) boyfriend of his mothers.

Ron's son was living with two recovering alcoholics, each with addictive personalities in a four bedroom detached house in a very nice area paid for by Ron, driving around in a car also paid for by Ron, receiving £840.00 per month from Ron which obviously was not being spent on Roger (thought he should now have a name), disability and carer's allowance again not being spent on Roger, nice life if you can get it !

Ron took Roger to Weston in February, four months into their new lives and routines, and the weather was bloody awful, Ron looked into his son's bag to pass him his coat and he didn't have one, Roger said he didn't have one at home either as he had grown out of his coats.

Next stop – kids clothes shop to buy a coat.

The pair braved the weather, and visited the pier and amusement arcade before heading off for something to eat. If any of you know Weston there is a very nice hotel on the sea front and the two of 'em headed in for some nosh.

The food was very good and Roger thinking he was Henry the eight let out an almighty burp which brought the restaurant to a standstill and silence, Roger looked at his Dad and turned around to see everyone looking at him he took a deep breath and said in a loud voice "pardon me" as he was nine years of age the people all said "Aaaah - good boy".

Ron was a little embarrassed but the other eaters had now moved on and were back to their earlier conversations or continuing with their meals.

On the drive back home, cold and wet, they both decided it would be nice to go somewhere warm so Ron booked a holiday in Tenerife for them both at the next half term holiday and set about finding or obtaining Roger's passport, his ex was her usual helpful self and she hadn't a clue where his passport was.

After spending almost a day on the telephone to the passport office Ron eventually had it sorted but had to go to Peterborough to collect it.

Half term, October, they set off for Tenerife, Ron is terrified of flying and settled himself down with a few large gin and tonics, Roger, a comic !

It was purely a sunshine holiday lazing about by the pool and enjoying a few cool beers and eating some nice grub, they stayed in one of the Princess chain of hotels and the surroundings could not have been any better with superb weather and glorious sunshine.

Ron began, their first day, to discover what it is like to be a single parent on holiday :-

Absolutely Fucking Brilliant............!

Women will do anything to help you, talk to you, assist with looking after your offspring, they obviously admire and respect Dad's who take their parental responsibilities seriously.

Walking to the pool for the first time on the first day a very attractive blond lady who was sunbathing on her own told Ron and Roger where to collect the sunbeds from and to put them by hers if they wished, Ron, missing the charms of the ironing lady didn't need asking twice.

Whilst lying there and swimming, the lady took interest and enjoyed swimming with Roger and Ron appearing to be really enjoying herself, Ron and her chatted and she said it was her final day at the resort and her friend had been sunburnt and had stayed in the room.

At the end of the day they went to their respective rooms to shower and change for dinner, they met again in the lift en route to the bar after dinner and Ron joked he didn't recognize her with her clothes on, she replied quite calmly "you can recognize me later if you would like"

Ron Roy Rogers

Music to Ron's ears and on that note Roger was despatched to bed, thankfully he was tired from the long flight and swimming all day!

No need to say anymore, is there?

Ron, was absolutely knackered on Day two of their holiday but he had a big smile on his face as they headed to the pool again, wondering what might happen today !

It was during this holiday Ron almost re named Roger as Rodney, they were enjoying a drink in the town one evening when a street seller approached them to see if he could sell them a watch, Roger looked at one which he liked and the seller asked for 40 euros, Ron bartered with him and it was reduced to 30, Ron stood firm and said 20 was the maximum Roger could afford as he only had 20 euros with him, the seller was just about to say he could have it for 20 when Roger spoke up and said "but Dad I have got 30 euros in my pocket"

Plonka!

Roger made some friends around the pool and thoroughly enjoyed his holiday making Ron happy seeing his son having fun, sadly nothing else exciting happened to Ron apart from enjoying female company, socially, at the poolside, dining room and bar.

Tenerife became an annual holiday for Ron and Roger at school half term breaks and they both looked forward to it for different reasons !

The summer arrived and Ronetta went with a friend to work the summer season in Greece and Ron's new home was nearing completion and whilst he was sad about leaving the rented home they had, he was looking forward to having his own house again.

Reg also had purchased a property and was moving out a couple of weeks before Ron.

The time of the move came and Ron with the help of his cousin, his son and son's friend, moved in on a Friday night which was rather emotional as all of the lights were switched on for the first time, the new furniture, T.V., bed linen, towels, cutlery etc., had all been delivered.

Ron had already christened every room in the house with the help of the ironing lady, even the garage on the bonnet of his Bentley!

The champagne was cracked open and yet another chapter in Ron's life was beginning.

Roger made friends in the village where Ron's house had been built and he thoroughly enjoyed his visits to dad's new home.

It was a few months before Christmas when they moved in and with the help of the ironing lady the Christmas Tree was erected and decorated, Christmas was strangely celebrated that year with Ron, his Parents, Ronetta and Roger.

Ron and Reg decided to spend the New Year abroad in the sunshine and were looking forward to jetting off the day after Boxing Day. However for Ron it almost didn't happen as his now ex-wife who on the day after Boxing Day had been taken to the Doctor's by Ronetta for a check up decided to jump out of Ronetta's moving car on the way home causing great distress to Ronetta, Ron was obviously very concerned about his daughter, his ex-wife had hobbled off and was obviously in her mind in a strange place and one feels that this was the start of her decline as she could see Ron was moving on with his life and in fact enjoying it, she obviously hated the idea of this as not only did she want to see Ron in the gutter during the divorce but she also wanted to jump up and down on him as he was lying there!

By the time Ron was in the Airport Lounge with Reg, his ex-wife had returned home slightly bruised and battered and Ronetta was at Ron's home with her Grandparents feeling extremely shocked at what had happened but at least Ron knew she was in safe hands.

During this break Ron and Reg met some new friends and had a thoroughly fabulous New Year and even ate sweatbreads at a champagne filled New Year Party, very strange to see Santa on the roof of a building when you are wearing shorts and teeshirt, or even swimming in the pool !

Ron had mentioned the decline of his ex and it was from this point on that she appeared to be more unstable than normal and this can only be attributable to the fact that Ron had moved on with his life and she hated the thought of him being happy.

Not long after this the Scottish boyfriend left her after apparently stealing all of her jewellery and some cash and returning to his beloved wife who rang Ron six months prior to this to ask him to have her husband "done over"!

The ex wife became more and more involved with the Born Again Christian gang, which Ron and the kids referred to as "The God Squad" who were a proper bunch of Tossers, and over a few months period she began to slide into a dark hole and it became apparent she needed psychiatric help as she was definitely beginning to lose the plot.

Ron worried for the safety of Roger as he was experiencing more than anyone, seeing her irrational and strange behaviour.

One Saturday evening when Roger was staying with Ron, Ron had a phone call at approximately Midnight from his ex saying her house was on fire. Ron is in no doubt whatsoever that she started the fire herself in order to attract attention and to obtain sympathy.

Luckily the Fire Brigade put out the fire and the Insurance Company dealt with the claim and put her and Roger into a hotel whilst the three months of repair and decoration took place.

Whilst staying at the hotel she met another man who was divorced and had children of a similar age to Roger and began a relationship with him.

Redemption Against the Odds

It was obviously doomed to fail from the beginning which it did after about six months putting Roger through her foolish mistakes, yet again, moving in with him part time and then full time and then part time again, shouting and arguing in front of the kids !

Roger had no stability or routine in his life, it was only when he was with Ron did he know where he was and what he was doing!

It was at this time that she was obviously deep inside this dark hole and attempted suicide by taking an overdose of tablets, however she was found by a friend (a recovering alcoholic and a born again Christian) and it was thought it was a cry for help and she was referred to the Psychiatric Department of the local hospital.

It appeared to help her receiving this treatment however no one could see inside her mind, people were unaware of the turmoil that she was in and she attempted to take her life again and was again discovered in the nick of time and it was decided by the authorities that she was sectioned, this process was sanctioned by her brother and she was taken in to a special mental health hospital.

At this time Roger obviously was staying with Ron and Ron's solicitor advised him to approach the

Courts for custody until such time as his ex wife was able to take care of herself and then she could have access to Roger when she became better.

The Courts agreed and Roger moved in with Ron.

Upon her release from hospital a month or so later and only allowed home because one of her "Born Again Christian" friends had promised to keep an eye on her and the hospital were also to phone her two/three times a day to make sure she was ok as she was on "suicide watch", she was released from hospital on a Thursday.

Two days later, early on Sunday morning, Ron having been out on the Saturday night for a few beers with friends was woken at 2.30am by the local Constabulary in fact two policemen arrived and were the two who had been involved in Ron's earlier appearances with the police force, the duty sergeant and the policeman who took him home.

Ron being quite concerned at their visit immediately asked if Ronetta, Roger and his parents were OK and he was assured they were but they had some bad news about his ex wife who had taken her own life sometime during the Saturday afternoon, the duty sergeant had to break the door to her house to gain entry.

Let's hope she has now found peace.

Redemption Against the Odds

Ron's solicitor who was unaware of what had happened, contacted him on Monday to tell him the pschyciatrist's report on his ex was carried out on the Wednesday before she left the hospital on Thursday, and had arrived at the solicitors office on Friday, this was all about his ex trying to regain custody of Roger because she obviously needed all of the money that came on a monthly basis as a result of her "looking after him"!

The report written by a registered and fully qualified pschyciatrist stated ....

"In my opinion Mrs. XXXX is fit and able to look after herself and there is no risk of self harm, and when she starts to look after Roger she will get better" !!!!!!!!!!!!!!!!!

Three days after this report being written and one day after receiving it – she had taken her own life.

What fucking chance do we all have, now Pschyciatrists can fuck up and get away with it.

So much for her "Born Again Christian Friend" who was supposed to be keeping an eye on her!

The hospital rang the police after they could not contact her and became concerned for her safety. Ron said to the Police he could not understand why they had come to tell him as she did have a brother and they should contact him, the Police Officers stated that in view of the past problems Ron had with her, they thought it best to tell him and for him to make sure the Children were OK.

Good, thoughtful, caring and considerate Coppers just the way they should be, and how they used to be.

Ron is a little unsure of what happened next but he went back to bed and slept till 9.30am the following morning, not feeling guilt, a little sadness maybe but an unexplainable feeling of relief as he realised there would not be any more trouble caused by her and no more pieces for him to pick up, so he thought, however he did not realise what a bloody mess she had made of things and the effect it would have on the children.

His first phone call was to his best mate Reg who was always ready with advice for Ron and always had an answer.

Ron told him what had happened and he asked Reg "How do I tell the kids"? his mate for once was stuck for words and uttered :-

"I don't fucking know"!

Where was the ironing lady now, when Ron needed someone?

Redemption Against the Odds

News travels quickly and as Ron was leaving his home the policeman who advised him to be very careful a year or more earlier as his ex was a very dangerous woman arrived to see how he was and to see if he needed any help with the kids.

What a gesture, Ron was gobsmacked as he didn't realise, after years of being told he was no good, useless, a wanker and a total waste of space, what people thought of him and for someone to be so nice, who he had met only once before in an unforgettable situation, this bowled him over!

Ron knew his daughter was staying with a friend and he travelled to the friend's house to break the news to his daughter, probably the hardest thing he has ever had to do in his life and luckily the friend's mother was a very nice person and helped him with Ronetta and looked after her whilst he went to his Parents house where Roger had stayed that Saturday night to also break the news to him, the 10 year old knew what Ron was about to say and tried to run out of the room.

After consoling him Ron took him home and Ronetta followed a little later on with a couple of her very close friends.

In fact Roger insisted they go to the Pub for Sunday lunch as they always did and it had a little park where they could play football which he insisted on playing, as though nothing at all had happened, an old footballing mate of Rons was in the pub and played with them to try to help the situation, a fabulous gesture because it nearly killed him, it was obviously Roger's way of coping with such a tragic situation, for a 10 year old and also his 18 year old sister to have to come to terms with.

His ex wife had left him and the children, in fact one each, a letter trying to explain why she had taken such drastic measures to end her life, Ron knows the answer to this and for the first time, he has never told anyone before, he now explains :-

His ex realised what an almighty mistake she had made by being so cruel, cheating, lying and divorcing him, and after she and the jock had split up she asked Ron to have her back and re-marry, Ron could not do this and could never forgive her selfish actions towards him and the children, she showed no consideration to any of them whilst she did for years, exactly what she wanted to.

This, Ron is convinced was the cause of her decline along with the brainwashing she received at AA and the Born Again Church, the drugs she was taking to wean her off the alcohol and the advice she was receiving from the so called friends and idiots with whom she had surrounded herself.

Once again Ron set about picking up the pieces and tidying up the bloody awful mess she had left behind.

All of the contents of Ron's ex's house were left to Ronetta and she has kept a number of items which she uses and has retained as memories, however as I am sure some of you may know, family and alleged friends begin to hover like vultures after the scraps, the God Squad friend who was supposed to be keeping an eye on her, asked for the cat as a memory, after six months she gave the fucking thing away!

Ron's ex's brother and his fourth wife took van loads of clothes, electrical equipment, furniture, ornaments, books and many other items, Ronetta at the time was very vulnerable and is unsure of what they actually took, but I know it was for their benefit and not Ronetta's.

Incidentally Roger and his mother stayed with her brother and his wife for a short time after the fire but were thrown out after an argument!

Nice people!

Her brother was also named in her will, receiving 20% of Ron's hard earned which has long since been wasted, along with everything else they had.

They are now, not surprisingly, divorced and fucking skint which is good enough for them!

For those of you who have had a divorce, you will be aware your solicitor recommends you to each make a will in case one of you "keels over" during the divorce, Ron and his wife agreed to each leave all to the the kids 50/50, of each other's respective estates so how on earth he got 20% is a fucking mystery, another one!

The drunk, who strangely enough was a Born again Christian, who found her the first time she attempted suicide rang Ron when he and Roger were in Tenerife on holiday to say she was starting an investigation into his ex's death because she couldn't understand how it had happened........!!!!!!

It was nothing to do with her, she was just an interfering busybody who had nothing better to do!

Ron told her in rather simple English if she ever did anything to bring this bloody awful mess back and put it in front of his kids it would be the last thing she ever did.

She didn't go ahead with the investigation!

Ron kept the letters for the kids and told them whenever they wanted to look at them they could, Ronetta waited a little while and Roger waited and looked at his letter when he was sixteen, which did not give him the answers he wanted, one day they both might understand, maybe if they ever read this book, they will.

Roger naturally struggled with the loss of his mom for a good few months but with the stability he now had along with a routine in his life he slowly began to cope reasonably well.

Before starting senior school he had to attend for a day to be introduced to the school and meet his new school pals with whom he would be spending time, upon arrival at the school Ron took time to speak with the secretary to explain Roger had in the last few weeks been through the traumatic experience of losing his mom and would she please mention this to the teacher in case he became a little upset. Obviously she didn't, and the teacher kept on about the kids obtaining their new uniform by visiting whatever school shop with their mother, Roger was not upset but found it quite funny that Ron was now his Mom as well as Dad, and to confirm this he sent his Dad a Mother's Day card!

Even Roger could force a smile, in what must have been a very difficult period for him

He started at senior school with his new uniform, in the village where they were now living and made more new friends, he and Ron developed a bond which under different circumstances may not have ever happened, they often ate out as Roger couldn't cope with Ron's cooking all of the time and met up with Reg regularly.

Ronetta seemed to cope too well, but Ron knew deep down she was broken up, hurt and angry and only time would allow it to come to the surface as Ron did not have any idea of what to do except to try to be a loving Dad!

She had a smashing group of friends and they would rally round each other and spent quality time with each other and obviously partying.

On one particular Saturday night they all jumped in a taxi and headed off to town to do what all nineteen/twenty year old girls do, they arrived back at one of the group's home in a taxi where they were all staying.

One of the girls decided she wanted to go back to her own home (approx. 1500 yards away) so:-

Guess who volunteered to drive her?

Guess what happened next?

Yep, you're right on both counts, Ronetta drove into a stationary expensive German car writing off her own twelve months old Peugeot, thankfully no one was injured or hurt.

Ronetta and her friend rang Ron at 2.00am in the morning to tell me they were ok, and both "sober" and what should they do?

As I was speaking to them I heard the police siren in the background !

She receieved a £400 fine and an eighteen month ban reduced to fourteen months if she attended a course about the dangerous effects of ALCOHOL, she could tell them more than they would ever know about the effects of alcohol, but decided against it.

As a result of this ban she headed off to Greece (after thanking Dad for paying her fine and solicitor's fees) again to work for the summer season with her close friend.

She returned later in the year and made Ron's weekend perfect as he did not know when she was arriving back home and a small family party ensued.

She soon got a job as she was a determined young lady and wanted to get on in life, and started going out with the girls again but Ron could tell she was not over losing her mother and whilst he did not expect her to ever fully get over it he thought she may have been accepting it a little better by now.

During this period of time Ron had two or three good friends apart from Reg who were in regular contact with him and helped him through it all, in fact one of them drove 400 miles from Scotland to see him and stayed over for a couple of nights and a few mcallum's were enjoyed at the bar, sadly he passed away a few years ago and Ron visits his grave every year up on the beautiful West coast of Scotland when visiting his family.

Before his passing he and Ron would meet up in Scotland and either watch a football game or enjoy having a catch up, meal and the customary malt or two, one night they were highly entertained by two businessmen and two "working ladies" who became louder as the evening wore on and also with the flowing champagne a lot raunchier, to the businessmen's delight!

At breakfast the following morning two rather sheepish looking men came from the lift and sat at a table near to us when one of them asked "what happened last night?" Tears of laughter came to Ron and his friend as these two men decided to leave the breakfast room !

A very dear friend and a gentleman who is constantly missed.

It was almost Christmas and Ron thought it best to try to make it different this year in view of events and plus, every Christmas in the past had always been troublesome with his ex's drinking and her family's behaviour.

He decided to have a barbeque on Christmas Day !

A gas barbecue was purchased and set up in the garage (with the door open) ready to cook Christmas lunch.

When the bbq was lit the flames were very weak and after checking it out the regulator from the gas bottle, given to Ron by a family friend who worked for a company supplying gas bottles and regulators, was faulty !

Ron knew there was one at his ex's house which had not been taken by the vultures so he set off with spanners to collect it and returned to cook a very different festive lunch which was enjoyed by all!

It was not all plain sailing though, as there was a smoke detector in the garage, being a new house the detector was powered, not by battery but by the main electricity supply and as the house was three storey there were detectors on each level plus the garage, bloody hell did it make a noise each time it was set off !

For a short while we were the neighbours from hell!

Ron waited at home on Boxing Day on his own as the ironing lady was calling in to see him, she never turned up and Ron was feeling very low by early evening, his telephone rang and it was the ironer's best friend who just happened to ring to see how he was and ask how Christmas went, she was divorced and obviously a little lonely so she jumped in a taxi and went to see Ron, after a few bottles of wine she stayed the night and a taxi took her home the following day, a little like the first Tenerife holiday, you never know what is going to happen next, not only does life have a way of sorting things out, it can also bring a big smile to your face when you least expect it.

Bet the ironing lady never knew about that !

A few weeks later it happened again and this time she brought a friend with her..!

Over the years Ron has found a number of people who he thought were close friends actually knew about the affair his drunken ex was having yet they chose not to say anything to him!

Ron cannot ever forgive these people fully and even now simply accepts and tolerates them, for a variety of reasons, but if ever Ron was aware of one of his friends being cheated on he would say something to that friend, it may spoil a friendship for a short while but if you have ever been on the receiving end of a cheat, We bet you wish someone had told you.

One of Ron's close friend's wife was fully aware of what his ex was up to whilst married to Ron but never said anything, and Ron's friend has said his wife never said anything to him about it...........?

Ron hopes this is true as he is very fond of his friend.

The friendship is continuing with them but Ron was hurt when he found out that she knew what was happening, it feels like a form of betrayal. Their son went through a very similar situation and Ron is certain they would have wanted someone to have told their son his partner was cheating on him..........!

Ron was also, around this time being screwed by two employees, and one in particular, we will call him Richard because he was and still is a proper Dick, he was shagging the receptionist at Ron's office who left her husband for him and had her 2 year old daughter in tow but Dick didn't have the balls to see it through and stayed with his wife, who would obviously put up with anything for whatever reason, only she could answer that and look at herself in the mirror?

Dick was just rude and nasty to his ex – lover and in everyone's interest it was best if one of them left as there was a terrible atmosphere at the office.

Ron smoothed the way for her to go and paid her for 2 months, to give her time to get another job, without having to struggle financially and to make sure her daughter was ok.

Dick did not give a damn as long as she was out of his way.

Ron also paid for a weekend away at a luxury hotel for Dick and his wife to try to sort out their marriage which must have worked as it is assumed they are still together, or has she just accepted the situation of him being a lying, cheating, no good bastard and just shuts up and puts up with it !

Redemption Against the Odds

Going back to a leopard not changing his spots, in his new job, we have been told he has been shagging another employee who has since left to have a baby – Dick's or her husbands?

In fact quite recently Ron has found out Dick used to pop around in an evening to see another lady who was the daughter of a client of Rons and who was going through a divorce at the time, her ex husband is now a client of Rons and he is looking forward to bumping in to Dick and knowing him it will be quite soon !

He obviously lacks any form of morals or scruples.

A legend in his own mind.

Dick was a greedy bastard when it came to money, he didn't think Ron would ever find out about him having cheques payable to his wife from customers, or paying refunds to customers in cash, which they received only a small part of, or none at all, bet they would love to know who they are, not only was he a cheat and a liar in his marriage but in his job as well!

In fact the name Dick sums him up very nicely and he deserves everything he has got coming to him, just remember Dick, be prepared, because.............

"IN THIS LIFE YOU ALWAYS HAVE TO PAY"

This does not just mean financially but in all ways.

Accepting and acknowledging the consequences of your actions can be very difficult especially for those who think very highly of themselves !

Ron had an old footballing mate called Ray who he had known for 40 years and he hated the sight of Dick, Ron always had to stop him from "Decking Dick" each time he saw him!

Hope you read the next book which, as mentioned earlier is underway as Dick's mistakes and errors make an entertaining read along with his lies, cheating, affairs and attempted affairs display him for what he really is !

His new business partner, as again mentioned earlier there were two of them working for Ron, is also better described but not for his stupidity or affairs, even though he thought of himself as a charmer with the ladies and tried it on with many of them, but more of his questionable business ethics?

Many things have since been brought to Ron's attention about both of their lack of business morals, scruples and ethics which are very disturbing and not what one expects from an employee in a position of trust.

Redemption Against the Odds

Going back to Ray who looked after Ron in Ron's early adulthood and Ron never forgot what he did for him!

He was a larger than life character and at 22 stone and 6' 7" once seen never forgotten and as you would expect he could take care of himself.

One night when he was working as a doorman at a local nightclub around 50 skinheads came to give him a good hiding as he had banned one of them the previous week for causing trouble.

As they chanted his name on the car park he walked out to them and quite calmly told them if they wanted to start to get on with it as he knew they would win but he told them he would make sure at least 3 or 4 of them would be seriously hurt!

Whilst they considered his proposal he offered to fight their best and if he won they would all leave with no more trouble being caused, they volunteered their best who was a karate black belt and a big fella, who agreed to it, as he was spinning around and high kicking you heard an almighty crack as Ray hit him only once on the jaw and knocked him spark out, they left the club car park and headed back to where they came from!

Ray spent a lot of his time in the last few years with Ron who took him on business trips and Ron and

Roger also took him on holiday a few years ago on their annual camping trip to North Wales and he loved every minute of it.

He had not been well and 6 months after their trip he passed away, Ron went to see him in hospital on Christmas Day which turned out to be the last time he saw him, it was extremely sad as he was in a lot of pain, at least now he is at peace and greatly missed.

CONCLUSION

Ron and Reg are still and always will be very close, this is due to everything they experienced over a very strange 10 year period in their lives, tears, laughter, highs and lows of business, family issues and a bond they will always have which is unbreakable along with a protective loyalty to each other.

They see each other every week and speak often and bounce ideas or problems off each other, Reg has always got some advice for Ron and never hesitates to offer it whether Ron wants it or not !

They each have new partners and life on a personal front is good for them (there is a life after all of the crap they went through and they also now have a future to look forward to)

They both have assets which one day they will be able to realise, when you consider their substantial divorce settlements they have both worked extremely hard to try to bounce back financially, however not in the present economic climate, and whilst it is good to have these assets you can't pay a bill with a brick ! so day to day business is continuing for both of them in their respective businesses.

It took time for both of them to move on and with the help of each other and their partners they have.

When they are together they sometimes talk about the past whether it be seriously or jokingly, but never morbidly, they have accepted their lot and now get on with it!

Reg is now a Grandad and along with his partner do their share of babysitting !

Ron is under pressure from his kids to re-marry and is at the moment giving this some serious thought as his partner of seven years has been like a breath of fresh air to him and the kids and given them something they never had before.

It is likely to happen in the near future, with Grandad as the best man !

A second marriage is the triumph of hope over experience.

For everyone who has gone through similar experiences there is a life to enjoy afterwards so don't despair and be prepared (the scouts motto) for the unexpected because you never know what is around the corner!

The old saying that Life is short is very true and it must be enjoyed even when times are bad and you think the whole world is against you and feel you can't go on.........YOU MUST......for the sake of the people who care about you and for yourself.

If Ron and Reg can do it anyone can, they have proven there is a life to look forward to even when you think there is not and you are at your lowest point do not give up, our two character's are normal hard working blokes who originate from council estates and with hard work, effort and a bit of luck, are still here to tell the tale, and intend on staying for a long while !

We bet you are wondering who the ironing lady is, or was, well you can keep on wondering, she was however a friend of Ron's who was full of good intentions and was always the life and soul of any party, but lacked any real conviction and was the type of woman who would go to the highest bidder, a very shallow person, not the sort of permanent partner you would want as she could never be trusted.

But she did have her good points and served a very satisfying purpose :-

IRONING !

Try to avoid situations where you need to show compassion, tolerance and patience, because you will not have any to offer !

Ron and Reg also achieved top marks in obtaining honours in their degrees from the University of Life!

Everyone sometimes needs a friend and luckily Ron and Reg had each other, if the only thing you have learnt from reading this book is the value and importance of friendship and family it has been worthwhile.

Friendship is not easy to maintain, it is a relationship where you have to work at being a good friend, you need acceptance because like in a marriage there are times when you will not always agree on matters but you must respect each other's views, again like in a marriage.

There are a lot of similarities in friendship and marriage and it proves if you work at both they can be fruitful and rewarding, they do however require both parties to participate!

Hopefully you will also realise it is not always the men who are at fault !

Look after your family, friends and particularly your best mate because you will miss them when they have gone!

At the start of this book Ron said "you need a mate" or a friend, and to elaborate a little on that statement.............

"A true friend is someone who knows who you are, understands where you have been and accepts what you have become."

Those who matter don't mind and those who mind don't matter!

The last word in this book appropriately reads

Ron Roy Rogers

The secret of a happy marriage
is and always will be :-

A Fucking Secret!

Good Luck to you all.

Best Wishes

Ron and Reg

Printed in Great Britain
by Amazon